The Monsters
Next Door

There are more books about the Bailey City Monsters!

The Monsters Next Door

by **Marcia Thornton Jones**
and
Debbie Dadey

illustrated by **John Steven Gurney**

A
LITTLE APPLE
PAPERBACK

SCHOLASTIC INC.
New York   Toronto   London   Auckland   Sydney

*To my friends
next door Anna Shafer,
Gayle Stoltz, Linda Jurgaitis,
Barb Baker, Andrea Marvel, and
Barb Green.—DD*

*To Kathleen and David Salas.
—MTJ*

ISBN 0-590-10787-9

Text copyright © 1997 by Marcia Thornton Jones and Debra S. Dadey.
Illustrations copyright © 1997 by Scholastic Inc.
All rights reserved. Published by Scholastic Inc.
LITTLE APPLE PAPERBACKS is a trademark of Scholastic Inc.
THE BAILEY CITY MONSTERS in design is a
trademark of Scholastic Inc.

12 11 10 9 8 7 6 5 4 3 2 1   7 8 9/9 0 1/0 2/0

Printed in the U.S.A.   40

First Scholastic printing, October 1997

Book design by Laurie Williams

Contents

1

Family from Freaksville

"Those are the weirdest people I've seen in my entire life," Annie whispered to her older brother, Ben. Annie and Ben were hiding behind a bush watching their new neighbors move into the brand-new house next door, 13 Dedman Street.

Ben rolled his eyes. "Can't you take a joke?" he asked, standing up to get a better view. "They're just dressed up for Halloween."

"Halloween is still a week away," Annie said. "These people are a family from Freaksville."

"I think they're cool," Ben said. "And that boy looks about my age."

Annie shuddered and looked at the oddly dressed trio. They were unloading boxes from a long, black station wagon that re-

1

minded Annie of a hearse. There was a tall, pale man with red hair wearing a long, black cape with a bloodred button holding it around his neck. The lady seemed normal enough, except for her hair. It stuck up like it was full of electricity. She had on a white doctor's coat, but it was covered with red, green, and purple stains.

The boy had a broad forehead and his hair was cut flat across the top of his head. He only needed bolts on his neck and Annie would have sworn he was Frankenstein's monster she'd seen on a late-night movie. He even wore the monster's ragged jeans and a shirt three sizes too small.

"I'd hate to meet that family in a dark alley," Annie said. "They give me the creeps."

"Speaking of creepy," Ben said, "here comes that monster teacher from school." A red-haired woman in a purple, polka-dotted dress walked down the sidewalk. Mrs. Jeepers taught one of the third-grade classes at Bailey Elementary. All of her students were convinced she was a vampire since she lived in a haunted house and wore a glowing green brooch. Most of the kids at school said the brooch was magic. Ben didn't believe it, but Annie did.

"I'm glad I'm in the other third-grade class," Annie said.

"Mrs. Jeepers must know them," Ben said as Mrs. Jeepers hugged each one of the newcomers before the whole group went inside the house.

Annie stood up from behind the bush. "If they know Mrs. Jeepers," she said, "then

there is something definitely wrong with them."

"Don't be such a baby," Ben told his sister. "Let's go see what they're doing."

Annie folded her arms in front of her chest. "I am not going to spy in their windows. It's not right."

"Fine," Ben said, "I'll do it without you."

Ben took off toward the house. Annie sighed and followed her brother. "I didn't think you were coming," Ben said.

Annie shrugged. "Somebody has to keep you out of trouble." Together they peeked into a large window in the side of the house. The lady with wild hair opened up a large box marked DUST.

"What kind of crazy people would bring dust with them?" Annie said.

"The kind that throw dust everywhere," Ben said. Annie and Ben watched in disbelief as the lady scattered dust all over the furniture the moving people had carried in.

"That lady is insane," Annie said. "Let's

get out of here before she turns us into giant dust bunnies."

Ben and Annie backed away from the window, but they didn't get far. A firm hand on Annie's shoulder stopped her dead in her tracks.

2
A Sticky Problem

"Aahhh!" Annie screamed.

Ben jumped back, ready to punch a monster in the chin. Instead, he stumbled over a bush and fell down right in the middle of the prickly branches.

A familiar face leaned over Ben and grinned. "Since when do you take naps in bushes?"

Annie grabbed her best friend's arm and giggled. "Jane, you scared us. We thought you were one of the new neighbors."

Jane and Annie had been best friends ever since Ben could remember. That was bad news for Ben since Jane was in his fourth-grade class. Jane pestered him all day at school, and then she and Annie ganged up on him at home.

"Help me up," Ben sputtered. "I think this is a thorn bush."

Jane rubbed her chin and acted like she was thinking very hard. "I'll make you a deal. You tell me what you were doing peeking in that window, and I'll help you up."

Ben took a deep breath. Jane was always trying to make deals.

"I'll make you a deal," Ben said. "You help me out and I won't beat you up."

Jane laughed. "Ben, you might scare all the little kids at school, but I know you're not as tough as you sound."

"Oh yeah? Just wait until I get out of this bush. I'll show you how tough I am." Ben kicked and wiggled until he was free of the sticky bush. The minute Ben stood up he lost his balance and fell back down.

"Not so fast," Jane said, looking down at her friend. "You haven't told me what you were up to."

"I don't have to tell you anything," Ben muttered.

"You do if you want out of that bush,"

Jane said, putting her hands on her hips. "Now, are you going to tell me or not?"

"I'll tell you," Annie offered.

"You be quiet," Ben warned. "Jane doesn't have to know everything."

"I do need to know if you want me to help you," Jane pointed out.

Ben thought about arguing some more, but he didn't like the way one of the branches was poking him in the arm. "This is like getting a booster shot with a tree trunk," he complained. "Okay, I'll tell you."

"Promise to tell the truth?" Jane asked.

"Don't I always?" Ben said.

Annie and Jane laughed. Ben never told the truth if he could help it. Jane held out her hand. "Shake on it," Jane ordered.

"Sure," Ben said with a lopsided grin, but instead of shaking Jane's hand he grabbed it and pulled. Jane landed beside Ben in the sticky bush.

"Oww!" Jane hollered. "That wasn't fair."

Annie giggled. "Of course it wasn't fair. Ben is never fair."

10

"Stop laughing," Jane begged, "and get me out of here."

"Perhaps I could help," said a strange voice with a thick accent.

Annie stopped laughing and turned around to face the strange voice. She gasped at what she saw.

3

Hauntly Manor Inn

The three friends froze as the new boy came around the corner of the house. He walked like his knees were frozen stiff. Every step with his heavy brown shoes left a deep footprint. When the boy reached the bush, he grabbed Ben's and Jane's arms and pulled. Both flew out of the bush, landing next to the strange kid. Annie noticed that the new neighbor was at least a head taller than Ben.

"Is sitting in the bushes an American custom?" the kid asked.

"N-No," Ben stammered. "Jane scared me and I fell. It's her fault."

"That's me," Jane said, sticking out her hand. Jane's knuckles cracked when the new kid shook her hand. "This is Ben and Annie. Are you from another country?"

"I am pleased to meet you," the new boy said. "My name is Kilmer Hauntly. I am from the Transylvanian Alps in Romania. My family and I noticed you watching us through the window. That is a strange way to meet neighbors. But then, everything about America is strange to me."

Annie's face turned red. "We shouldn't have looked in your windows. But we really wanted to meet you."

Kilmer grinned. "Please, do come in. My family wants to meet you, too." Kilmer walked toward the front door.

"Do you think it's safe?" Annie whispered to her brother.

"Of course it's safe," Ben said, but he didn't sound very sure.

Ben, Jane, and Annie followed Kilmer to the front of the house. They already knew the way. The house was brand-new and the kids had explored the empty rooms before the Hauntlys moved in. It was the biggest house on Dedman Street and it still smelled like wet paint.

14

Kilmer stopped just inside the door to pet a black cat perched on a stool.

"What a cute kitty," Annie said. She reached out to pet the cat, but Kilmer stopped her.

"Sparky is not very friendly," he said.

Just then, Sparky's yellow eyes grew round as she stared down the empty hall. She hissed, arched her back, and raced through a door.

Ben laughed. "Sparky looks like she just saw a ghost."

Annie and Jane giggled, but Kilmer didn't even smile. Instead, he led the three kids into the living room. The lady with the stained coat was opening another box that had the word WEBS scribbled on the side. The DUST box was empty and a fine layer of dust covered everything in the room.

"This is my mother, Hilda," Kilmer said.

Kilmer's mother looked like she had been dipped in milk. Her skin was as white as her teeth and her wild hair. "She is a sci-entist," Kilmer said. Ben, Jane, and Annie all smiled at their new neighbor. "We moved here because she got a job at FATS."

Annie knew that FATS was a big scientific lab at the edge of Bailey City. The initials stood for Federal Aeronautics Technology Station. Annie gulped and wondered what kind of scientist Hilda Hauntly was.

"Your auntie Jeepers was right," Hilda told Kilmer. "She said you would have plenty of friends in Bailey City." Then Hilda called into another room. "Boris, come meet Kilmer's new friends."

Boris Hauntly looked like his feet never touched the floor as he glided into the room, his black cape flowing behind him. Annie gulped when she saw Boris' slime-green eyes.

"What a delicious treat," Boris said, licking his lips. He spoke with the same thick accent as Kilmer and Hilda.

Jane held out her hand. "Welcome to the neighborhood," she said as Boris shook her hand.

Boris grinned so big his pointy eyeteeth

16

showed. Then he spread out his hands and said in a booming voice, "Welcome to Hauntly Manor Inn, a bed-and-breakfast hotel for weary travelers from all over the world."

"Hauntly Manor Inn?" Annie said in a squeaky voice.

Boris nodded. "And you shall be our special guests this Friday evening. We will have a party!"

"Then we must hurry," Hilda said. "This house is not decent for receiving guests."

"Remember to come back Friday," Boris said as he ushered the three kids to the front door, "as soon as the sun sets."

4
Fair and Square

"How about a game?" Jane asked Annie and Ben the next afternoon. Jane carried her old dirty soccer ball into their backyard.

"Let's play boys against girls," Annie said. "We'll beat Ben fair and square."

"Two against one is not fair," Ben argued. "We need another boy." Then he slapped his forehead. "And I know just where to find one."

Ben, Annie, and Jane jogged next door to the Hauntlys'. Ben lifted the tarnished door knocker and let it fall. Moments later, they heard heavy footsteps echoing through Hauntly Manor. The door slowly opened.

Kilmer smiled. "Please," he said in his strange accent, "come in."

Ben shook his head. "Would you like to play soccer?" he asked. "I need you for my team."

Jane laughed. "He'll need more than you," she said. "Ben is the worst player in Bailey City."

"Am not," Ben argued. He patted Kilmer on the shoulder and said to him, "I bet together, we could beat their socks off."

Kilmer frowned. "But I do not know how to play," he told Ben.

"No problem," Ben said. "I'll teach you everything you need to know."

The four kids gathered at the dead end part of Dedman Street and started to play. Kilmer tried to catch up to the ball, but he wasn't used to playing soccer.

Soon, Annie and Jane were winning and Ben got desperate. He side-kicked the ball all the way to Kilmer. Kilmer gave the ball a mighty kick. Ben, Annie, and Jane stopped dead in their tracks when the ball zoomed straight into the goal.

"All right," Ben said, doing a little victory dance. "That's the way to play. Kilmer and I are a great team!"

"It won't do you any good," Jane said, pointing. Kilmer had kicked the ball so hard, it popped. Now the ball was as flat as a pizza.

"That was an old ball anyway," Ben said with a grin. "Next time we'll use my new one."

Annie picked up the flat ball. "This reminds me. Mom said we could decorate our pumpkins today."

"Decorate pumpkins?" Kilmer asked.

"We always paint faces on our pumpkins and make them look really eerie," Annie said.

Kilmer nodded. "That sounds like something my family would enjoy."

"Come on," Ben said. "I'll show you how to make a great painted jack-o'-lantern."

The kids spent the rest of the afternoon decorating pumpkins. When they finished, they admired their work.

Annie's pumpkin had a big grin. Jane's

pumpkin had a crooked frown. Ben's pumpkin was so messy you couldn't tell what it was. But Kilmer's pumpkin looked like something out of a monster movie, complete with pointy fangs.

"That's the scariest pumpkin I've ever seen," Annie said. "How did you think of a face like that?"

Kilmer shrugged. "I just thought about one of my cousins. Maybe he'll come to visit someday." Kilmer walked home to perch his painted jack-o'-lantern on Hauntly Manor's porch.

Annie shuddered. She hoped she'd never see anybody who looked as scary as Kilmer's pumpkin.

5

Halloween

"We're going to Burger Doodle for a milk shake," Annie said after school a few days later. "Do you want to come?" Ben, Annie, and Jane were standing beside the jungle gym with Kilmer.

"Then we're going to play soccer," Ben said. "With you on my side, we can beat the pants off Annie and Jane again."

Kilmer shook his head. "I must do my homework and help make the inn ready." Kilmer looked both ways and crossed Forest Lane. Annie, Ben, and Jane followed him as he turned down Dedman Street.

"You've been going to Bailey Elementary for three whole days," Ben said to Kilmer, "and we've only played soccer once. Don't you think it's time to have some fun?"

Kilmer grinned at Ben. "I am having fun getting ready for the party."

Kilmer's cat, Sparky, was perched on the Hauntly Manor porch railing. Her yellow eyes watched Kilmer wave to the three kids. The cat continued to stare at the kids even after Kilmer disappeared inside the front door.

"I can't wait until Friday," Jane said. "I already have my costume. I'm going to be a ghost."

Annie grinned. "I'm going to be a princess. I just have to finish making my crown."

"Do you think the Hauntlys know that Friday is Halloween?" Jane asked.

"Of course they do," Ben said. "That's why they're having a party."

"Strange," Annie said. "Kilmer never mentioned Halloween."

"That's not the only strange thing," Jane said. "Have you noticed Hauntly Manor lately?"

"What about it?" Annie asked.

"Well," Jane said slowly, "when the Hauntlys moved in last weekend that house was brand-new. Now look at it. Houses don't turn old that fast."

Jane was right. Two shutters were lopsided and a jagged crack reached across one of the living room windows. The railing leading up to the porch was falling apart and the tree in the front yard had died. Even the grass had turned from bright green to a sickly shade of dirty brown.

"This place is creepy," Ben admitted.

"Worse," Jane said. "It looks downright haunted!"

"Don't be silly," Annie said. "Houses have to be old to have ghosts."

"Unless," Ben said, looking at the black cat on the porch, "ghosts moved in."

"With vampires," Jane added, "and mad scientists."

Annie adjusted her backpack and looked at Jane. "What are you talking about?"

27

"You have to admit the Hauntlys are unusual," Ben said.

"So are you," Annie said. "But that doesn't make you a goblin."

"Remember Hilda?" Jane argued. "She's as pale as a ghost and she always wears that lab coat with weird stains."

"Boris' eyeteeth make him look like Dracula's cousin," Ben added. "After all, they are from Transylvania. Isn't that where Dracula is from?"

"What about Kilmer?" Annie asked.

Jane sat her backpack on the sidewalk. "Maybe Kilmer's an experiment Hilda cooked up in her lab."

"You're crazy," Annie said. "The Hauntlys seem strange to us because they're new to this country."

"Then how do you explain a brand-new house turning into a haunted house?" Jane asked.

Annie laughed. "It's for the party," she said. "Friday is Halloween."

Just then, Sparky arched her back and

hissed. Then she darted around the house as if a monster were chasing her tail.

Jane took a deep breath. "I hope you're right," she told Annie. "Or we're in for the Halloween surprise of our lives."

6

Monster Movies

On Halloween evening Ben, Annie, and Jane walked with Kilmer to meet a group of other Bailey School kids at the mall.

Annie wore a long pink dress with a sparkling crown. Jane had on a bedsheet with two holes in it for her to see through. Ben had wrapped himself in white rags to look like a mummy. Kilmer looked like he always did. He wore heavy brown shoes, jeans, and a shirt that was too small.

"I can't wait until your party," Annie told Kilmer.

"We'll go right after trick or treating at the mall," Jane said. "It'll be dark by then."

"I am sure it will be fun," Kilmer said to his new friends. "But why did you tell me to bring this pillowcase?" He held up a case as black as the night sky.

"For all your treats," Annie told him.

"You probably always used plastic bags," Ben said. "But I learned a long time ago that pillowcases hold more loot."

A large group of Bailey School kids were already at the mall. The Bailey Elementary principal, Mr. Davis, was dressed up as Humpty Dumpty.

Kilmer smiled when he saw all the costumes. "Ah," he said, "this reminds me so much of my home in Transylvania."

The big group of kids went to every shop in the mall. Each store gave treats to the kids.

"Mega Ghost Bubble Balls," Ben hollered, "my favorite!"

"I'll make you a deal," Jane said. "I'll trade you my Mega Balls for your suckers."

"It's a deal," Ben said, "if you throw in your licorice and chocolate-covered pretzels."

"Fine," Jane said. "I don't like those anyway."

After Ben, Annie, and Jane finished trading, the four kids hurried to the center of the mall. They got there just in time for the costume contest. Annie giggled when Kilmer won first prize for best costume, but Ben didn't laugh. He was mad because Kilmer's bag had more treats in it. In fact, Kilmer had more treats than anybody.

"Don't be mad," Kilmer told him. "You can have mine. I really do not like candy."

"You don't like candy?" a girl named Liza asked. Liza and her friends Howie, Melody, and Eddie were in Mrs. Jeepers' third-grade class at Bailey Elementary.

Kilmer shook his head. "The treats my mother makes are much better. You will see when you come to my house. You are all invited."

"But we can't go yet," Liza's friend Eddie griped. "The theater is showing monster cartoons."

Kilmer smiled before walking away. "Meet me at my house after the cartoons. We are planning a great party!"

It was dark when the movie let out. The

kids hurried down Forest Lane. As soon as they turned onto Dedman Street a chilling wind sent dead leaves scurrying at their feet. Jane and Annie glanced over their shoulders to make sure no monsters lurked in the shadows.

Annie looked up at the bare tree branches. They reminded her of long bony fingers, blowing in the wind. Annie expected one of the branches to grab her any minute. But the branches didn't grab Annie, they grabbed Ben.

"You're coming undone." Annie giggled as one of the branches snagged Ben's costume. A long piece of Ben's white rag fluttered in the wind.

"Fix it," Ben ordered Annie.

"I'd be glad to tie you up," Jane interrupted. She hurried to fix Ben's costume before the wind unraveled it all.

When Ben stopped in front of the Hauntly Manor Inn, Melody gulped and said, "Is that where Kilmer lives?"

The group of Bailey School kids peered

up at the black windows of Hauntly Manor. A loose shutter banged against the paint-chipped wall and wind moaned through the dead tree branches in the front yard. Dozens of eerie jack-o'-lanterns flickered on the Hauntlys' front porch. Annie was sure she heard a werewolf howling in the distance.

Jane nodded. "I told you their house was creepy."

"It's worse than creepy," Howie said. "It looks like something out of the monster movie we just saw."

Annie pointed to the dark windows. "It doesn't look like anybody is home," she said.

"They must be home," Jane told her. "The Hauntlys have been planning this party for days."

"It looks quiet," Ben said. "Deathly quiet."

"Maybe we shouldn't go in there," Liza said. Annie nodded in agreement.

"Are you out of your mind?" Eddie asked. "Kilmer said his mother's treats are better than candy. I'm not about to miss out on them."

"Then you're not afraid to go first?" Melody asked.

"I'm not afraid," Eddie said, "if Ben's not afraid."

Eddie and Ben looked at each other. It was a known fact that Eddie and Ben were always trying to prove who was the toughest kid in Bailey City.

"I'm not afraid," Ben told him.

"Me neither," Eddie said. But Eddie and Ben didn't move until Jane gave them a shove.

The group of kids slowly followed Ben and Eddie up the creaking steps to the Hauntly Hotel. Together, Ben and Eddie lifted the heavy metal knocker and let it fall against the wooden door. A loud knock echoed within.

Slowly, the door creaked open.

7
Beethoven's Ghost

Boris Hauntly sent chills up the kids' backs when he opened the door. "Welcome to Hauntly Manor Inn," he said in a deep voice.

Annie took one look at Boris as the full moon shone on his slime-green eyes and almost fainted. "I'm not going in there," Annie whispered to Jane.

Jane nodded. "You're right," she said. "Let's get out of here." But before they could run, the whole group of kids squeezed through the door, pushing Jane and Annie inside Hauntly Manor. Boris closed the heavy door with a loud thud.

"Trapped," Annie whispered with a gulp.

"Wow," Ben said, "we like what you've done with the place."

Boris smiled, showing his huge pointy eyeteeth. "Yes, it feels very homey now."

The kids looked around. It looked anything but homey to them. The inside of the house was painted red, bloodred. A thick layer of dust covered heavy antique furniture and cobwebs clung in every corner. Huge candelabras filled with fat, dripping candles were the only light in the spooky house. As Boris showed them into the living room, Annie felt like she was in her worst nightmare.

"Phe-ew!" Eddie said rudely. "It smells like something died in here."

Liza squeezed Eddie's shoulder. "Be quiet," she whispered. "Don't you know who that is?"

"Of course I do," Eddie snapped. "That's Kilmer's dad."

Liza squeezed Eddie's arm so hard he jumped. "That's Boris Hauntly. He's Mrs. Jeepers' brother. We met him at Mrs. Jeepers' family reunion."

Eddie looked at Boris and nodded. At the reunion, Eddie and his friends Liza, Melody, and Howie had all thought Boris was a vampire bat. Now he was living here in Bailey City. Eddie pulled his costume up over his neck.

Annie jumped and grabbed Ben's arm when a huge pump organ in the corner of the room started playing loud, creepy music. "Oh my gosh," she told Ben, "there's nobody playing the organ."

Ben looked. Sure enough, the keys were being pressed down, but the organ bench was empty. "Maybe the ghost of Hauntly Manor likes Beethoven," Ben joked.

But Ben wasn't smiling when Hilda swept into the room and greeted the children. Her eyes looked just as wild as her spiky hair. When she shook Ben's hand, Ben felt like he was touching a dead woman. Hilda's hand was bony and cold, stone cold.

The entire group of kids huddled together in the middle of the living room, staring at the strange pictures on the wall,

when a loud clomping noise sounded over the organ music.

Clomp. Clomp. CLOMP.

"What's that?" Annie asked Ben nervously.

Ben gulped. "I don't know. But it's getting closer."

8
Burying Things

Kilmer stomped into the room with his heavy shoes. "Welcome!" he told the kids. "Would you like a tour of Hauntly Manor?"

Annie shook her head, but no one noticed. Kilmer grabbed her hand and dragged her into the hall. Kilmer's grip was so strong, Annie had no choice but to follow him. Ben and Jane hurried to catch up while the other kids gathered around the organ in the living room.

"Let me show you the conservatory," Kilmer said.

"What's a conservation?" Ben asked Jane.

"He said conservatory, noodle brain," Jane told Ben.

"So, since you're so smart, what's a conservatory?" Ben asked.

Jane shrugged. "I think it's a place to put your bottles and cans for recycling."

Kilmer led the group into a glass room. The glass walls were lined with hundreds of clay pots filled with withered brown plants. In the center of the room lay four long flower beds piled with mounds of rich black soil. "How nice to have a room just to grow plants," Annie told Kilmer.

Kilmer nodded. "My father is an active gardener. He loves burying things in the

soil. He even brought this special dirt all the way from Transylvania."

Ben poked Jane in the arm. "I don't see any recycling bins in here."

Jane stuck out her tongue at Ben. "Maybe Boris is recycling dead bodies instead of paper," she said softly.

Annie looked at the dying plants. "I'm sure the plants will be beautiful once they've recovered from moving," she told Kilmer.

Kilmer looked at Annie in a funny way. "My father thinks they are beautiful just like this."

Annie didn't say anything, she just followed Kilmer into the next room. "This is my mother's laboratory," Kilmer explained.

"Cool," Ben said as he looked around the cluttered room. Test tubes of every size and shape lined black countertops. A nearby beaker oozed with thick green bubbles.

Ben reached out his hand to grab one of the test tubes, but Kilmer stopped him. "Don't touch that," Kilmer warned. "My mother has some very strong chemicals in here. There's no telling what they might do to you."

Ben pulled his hand back and nodded. Jane tapped Ben on the shoulder. "I'll make you a deal," Jane said. "You drink one of those and I won't bother you for a week."

"No way," Ben said. "I might be turned into some kind of monster."

Jane giggled. "You couldn't be any worse of a monster than you already are."

"You're about as funny as bat poop," Ben said, rolling his eyes at Jane.

Jane and Ben had to hurry as Kilmer took Annie out of the laboratory. Annie still heard the organ playing in the living room, but she heard something else, too. It was a low growling sound.

"What's that funny noise?" she asked Kilmer.

"I hear nothing unusual," Kilmer told her.

The growling grew louder. "I didn't know you had a dog," Annie said.

"A dog? Sparky would never allow us to have a dog. Now, here's the kitchen," continued Kilmer. Then he led them into the strangest room they'd ever seen.

9
Eyeballs

Jane gasped. Annie whimpered and grabbed Ben's arm. The rest of the kids had left the living room and were huddled in a corner of the kitchen. They were staring at Boris with wide eyes. Boris stood in front of a huge door of an iron stove. He was using a sharp poker to stoke up flames. Fire shot up all around him, making him look like he was on fire. In fact, the red painted walls made the whole room look like it was on fire. Gray smoke billowed out of a black cauldron sitting on top of the ancient stove.

"The stove must be a bazillion years old," Annie blurted.

Kilmer nodded. "It has been in my family since the beginning of time."

Boris used a long wooden spoon to stir whatever was in the cauldron. Then he

turned and smiled at the crowd of kids. Jane couldn't help noticing his pointy eye-teeth.

"You're just in time for a special Hauntly Manor Inn treat," Boris told the kids. "Who's hungry?"

Eddie's and Ben's hands shot into the air. "I'm starved," Ben yelled.

Kilmer pulled Ben over to the stove. "My dad cooked up something extra special for my new friends. You can be the first to sample some of these great broiled lizard tongues."

Boris held out a tarnished silver tray loaded with red and pink strips. Ben took one look at the tongues and lost his appetite.

"Go ahead," Kilmer told Ben, "they're delicious."

Ben gulped. "That's okay. I'll let Eddie go first."

Eddie frowned. "What else do you have to eat?" he asked.

"We have a feast," Boris told the kids. He

waved his hand toward a huge wooden
table.

"All of my favorites!" Kilmer said, pointing to several trays. "Roasted skeleton
knuckles, fried rat claws, and boiled buzzard eyeballs."

The kids looked at Eddie. He didn't
move. They looked at Ben. His face was as
white as his mummy costume. Just then a
strange sound came from upstairs. It
sounded like huge claws scratching on the
floor above them.

"W-What's that?" Annie stammered.

"That's probably the skeletons coming to get their knuckles back," Ben joked.

But nobody laughed because just then the howling began. "Let's get out of here!" Melody screamed.

The kids dashed away from Kilmer and Boris, pushing Jane, Annie, and Ben with them. They didn't stop running until they reached the shadows of the dead tree.

"Why did you run?" Jane asked.

"Didn't you hear that monster?" Liza whimpered. "It was coming to get us."

Ben laughed. "This is Halloween, you pumpkinhead. That was just a spooky tape."

"What about the rat claws, skeleton knuckles, and buzzard eyeballs?" Howie said. "There's something very strange going on here."

"Of course there is," Jane said. "After all, it is Halloween."

"Halloween at the Hauntlys is anything but normal," Eddie said.

"You guys are crazy," Ben said.

"Not as crazy as you," Melody said. "I'm going for help."

Then the gang of kids raced down Dedman Street, leaving Annie, Ben, and Jane standing alone in the dark under the dead tree.

10
Nothing but Trouble

"We have to do something," Ben told Jane and Annie. They huddled under the dead tree in the Hauntly Manor yard. A full moon cast eerie shadows across the lawn.

"I plan to," Jane said. "I'm going home and eating candy until I'm sick."

Annie grabbed Jane's arm. "How can you think of eating after seeing buzzard eyeballs and rat claws?"

"Those weren't real," Jane argued. "I'm sure they were just for Halloween."

"Eddie thought they were real enough to go for help," Annie said. "I bet they'll run the Hauntlys out of town."

"We can't let that happen to Kilmer," Ben said. "He's the only other boy on this block."

Jane tugged off her ghost costume and stuffed it into her bag of candy. "Who cares about Kilmer?" she said. "The two of you together are trouble anyway."

Ben grinned. "Exactly. I'm not about to let the best thing that happened to Dedman Street get chased out of town by a little squirt like Eddie."

"You're going to be in trouble if you mess with Eddie," Annie said.

"Eddie doesn't scare me," Ben said. "Besides, with the Hauntlys on our side we'll never have to worry again."

"But what about Boris and Hilda?" Jane asked. "I don't like having monsters for neighbors."

"You shouldn't call Boris and Hilda monsters," Annie said. "They may be a little different, but that doesn't mean they should be run out of town."

"Annie's right for once," Ben said. "And it's up to us to help them. Come here and I'll tell you my plan."

Jane and Annie gathered close to Ben,

but before Ben could say another word Boris glided out the front door. Hilda and Kilmer followed close behind.

"Ben," Kilmer called. "Please come back and have some treats."

Hilda put her long bony fingers on Annie's arm. "Is there a problem?" Hilda asked Annie. "Everyone left so suddenly."

"There's a problem," Ben blurted out, "a big problem. Let's get inside before somebody sees us and we'll tell you all about it."

"Can't you shut that racket up?" Ben asked Kilmer about the loud organ music as everyone settled into the dusty living room. Instantly, the organ stopped playing and Hauntly Manor became deathly still.

"How'd you do that?" Annie asked softly.

Kilmer smiled. "We have a very talented organ."

Ben wanted to ask Kilmer about the organ, but he knew he didn't have a moment to waste. Ben told the Hauntlys all about Halloween.

When Ben finished, Boris scratched his head. "Explain this again," Boris asked Ben.

"Every year kids dress up as monsters and ghosts," Ben said.

"And princesses," Annie interrupted.

Ben frowned at Annie and continued. "It's a chance to pretend to be whatever we want to be. But the best part is getting lots and lots of treats."

"You mean like boiled eyeballs and roasted skeleton knuckles?" Kilmer asked.

"No, no," Jane said. "In Bailey City, we like candy and junk food. Nobody wants healthy stuff for Halloween."

Hilda Hauntly shook her head. "What a strange custom."

"We must find a costume," Boris told his family, "before the others return."

Jane held up her hand. "No, believe me. You're fine just the way you are."

"We need to get some of this junk food and candy for our guests," Hilda said.

"You can use some of my candy," Annie

said. She dumped her candy onto the thick black rug.

Jane dug through Annie's candy bars, suckers, and candy corn. "This won't work. Not a single thing looks like buzzard eyeballs or rat claws," she pointed out.

"Listen," Annie said. "I think I hear Eddie and the rest of the kids outside. We'd better think of something and fast."

Jane pawed through her own bag of candy. "I don't have anything that will work, either."

Boom. Boom. Boom. "They're banging on the door," Annie said with a gulp. "What are we going to do?"

Ben darted toward the kitchen with his bag of candy. "Let them in," he yelled over his shoulder. "Leave the rest to me."

11

Trick or Treat?

Boom. Boom. Boom.

"Okay," Ben said as he came out of the kitchen. Ben, still dressed in his mummy costume, held a huge tray. "Open the front door."

"Maybe you shouldn't," Annie said. "They sound awfully mad."

"Don't worry about a thing," Ben told them. "I have it all under control."

The door creaked as Boris slowly pulled it open. "Happy Halloween," he said in his strange Transylvanian accent.

The crowd gasped and stepped back — everybody, that is, but Principal Davis. "Please come in and have some treats," Hilda said politely.

Eddie peeked from behind Principal

Davis. "Go ahead and ask them about the eyeballs."

Ben grinned. "Sure, we have plenty of eyeballs and rat claws, too." And then, Ben, the mummy, stepped in front of Boris and held up the tray. It was piled high with white bubblegum balls and chocolate-covered pretzels.

"What about the broiled lizard tongues?" Melody asked.

Annie pointed to a mound of long stringy licorice. "Here they are. Don't you want some?"

Eddie folded his arms over his chest. "You guys are tricking us."

"We're just trying to give you a treat," Jane laughed. "I'll make you a deal. You have a treat and we'll never tell anyone what a big chicken you were this Halloween at the Hauntlys'."

Ben gave the tray to Kilmer and flapped his wings. "*Bawk. Bawk. Bawk.*"

Principal Davis scratched his bald head.

"I think you children have had enough excitement for one night. I know I have." Principal Davis disappeared down Dedman Street after apologizing to the Hauntlys.

The rest of the kids stared at the Hauntlys. "You're not getting away with this," Eddie said.

"Oh no?" Ben asked with a smile.

Just then the organ blasted out a haunting melody, and a piercing howl echoed from the attic of Hauntly Manor.

Two girls screamed and Eddie's face turned as white as Ben's mummy costume.

"Let's get out of here while we still can!" Liza screamed.

12

One Too Many Monsters

The whole group of kids raced down Dedman Street, while Ben and Kilmer laughed.

"That was pretty cool," Ben said to Kilmer. "How'd you get the organ to play?"

Kilmer just smiled. "It's an old family secret," he told his new friends. "We have lots of them."

"Whew," Annie told Jane and Ben when they left the Hauntlys'. "That was close."

"I can't believe you were going to give your candy to Eddie," Jane told Ben.

Annie agreed. "You like candy more than cartoons. You must have really wanted to help Kilmer."

"It's nice having someone to play soccer with," Ben said. "Besides, it was cool when the Hauntlys scared the other kids. I like having the Hauntlys on our side."

Jane shrugged. "It figures that Ben would be the only kid in Bailey City to make friends with a Frankenstein monster. After all, Ben is part monster himself."

Ben held out his arms in front of him like a mummy and walked with stiff legs toward Jane. "I am a monster," Ben said in his creepiest voice.

"I think there are too many monsters on Dedman Street," Jane said. "But I can take care of that."

She snatched a tattered end of Ben's costume and pulled hard. With a little shove from Annie, Ben twirled around and around. His rags unraveled and fell to the ground.

Annie giggled. "That's one less monster around here. But what are we going to do about having the Hauntlys for neighbors? Jane was right about them. I don't know if I'll like having monsterlike people living next door."

"You better get used to it," Ben warned. "I don't think they're going anywhere. Didn't Boris say he was making their house into a bed-and-breakfast?"

"That's right," Annie said. "But who would stay at a monster motel?"

Jane gulped. "Monsters, that's who. Lots and lots of monsters."

Just then the clouds drifted over the full moon and the kids found themselves in total darkness. Wind rattled through bare tree branches, and a howl from the Hauntlys' attic cut through the night.

"We may be in trouble," Annie said. "Big trouble."

About the authors

Marcia Thornton Jones and Debbie Dadey like to write about monsters. Their first series with Scholastic, **The Adventures of the Bailey School Kids,** has many characters who are *monster-ously* funny. Now with the Hauntly family, Marcia and Debbie are in monster heaven!

Marcia and Debbie both used to live in Lexington, Kentucky. They were teachers at the same elementary school. When Debbie moved to Aurora, Illinois, she and Marcia had to change how they worked together. These authors now create monster books long-distance. They play hot potato with their stories, passing them back and forth by computer.

About the illustrator

John Steven Gurney is the illustrator of **The Bailey City Monsters** and **The Adventures of the Bailey School Kids**. He uses real people in his own neighborhood as models when he draws the characters in Bailey City. John has illustrated many books for young readers. He lives in Vermont with his wife and two children.